How the
Leopard
Got His Spots

Retold by Elizabeth Rogers

Illustrated by Petra Brown

FRANKLIN WATTS
LONDON•SYDNEY

First published in 2010 by
Franklin Watts
338 Euston Road
London
NW1 3BH

Franklin Watts Australia
Level 17/207 Kent Street
Sydney
NSW 2000

Text © Franklin Watts 2010
Illustration © Petra Brown 2010

A CIP catalogue record for this book is available
from the British Library.

ISBN 978 0 7496 9404 3 (hbk)
ISBN 978 0 7496 9410 4 (pbk)

Series Editor: Jackie Hamley
Series Advisor: Catherine Glavina
Series Designer: Peter Scoulding

Printed in China

Franklin Watts is a division of
Hachette Children's Books,
an Hachette UK company.
www.hachette.co.uk

This Just So story is
based on a tale written
by an author called
Rudyard Kipling over
a hundred years ago.

Just So stories give fun
ideas for why different
animals are like they are.

Long ago, all the animals
were the same colour.

Leopard hunted
Giraffe and Zebra.

He could see them, but
they could not see him.

One day, Giraffe and Zebra went into the forest.

They changed colour
with the shadows
and the sunshine.

9

"Where's my dinner?"
asked Leopard.

"In the forest!"
said Baboon.

Leopard could smell Giraffe and Zebra, but could not see them.

"Where are they?"
he cried.

Leopard soon caught
something that smelled
like Zebra, but he could
not see it.

14

Zebra ran off laughing.
"I've changed!" he said.

"Then I must change too, so you cannot see me!" said Leopard.

Leopard's skin soon
began to change.

And that's how
Leopard got his spots.

Puzzle Time!

a
b
c
d
e
f

Put these pictures in the right order and tell the story!

cheeky

spotty

stripy

hungry

Which words describe Leopard and which describe Zebra?

Turn over for answers!

Notes for adults

TADPOLES are structured to provide support for newly independent readers. The stories may also be used by adults for sharing with young children.

Starting to read alone can be daunting. **TADPOLES** help by providing visual support and repeating words and phrases. These books will both develop confidence and encourage reading and rereading for pleasure.

If you are reading this book with a child, here are a few suggestions:

1. Make reading fun! Choose a time to read when you and the child are relaxed and have time to share the story.
2. Talk about the story before you start reading. Look at the cover and the blurb. What might the story be about? Why might the child like it?
3. Encourage the child to retell the story, using the jumbled picture puzzle as a starting point. Extend vocabulary with the matching words to characters puzzle.
4. Talk about how the story has fun with how different animals look, and see if you can think of other animals and why they might look the way they do.
5. Give praise! Remember that small mistakes need not always be corrected.

Answers

Here is the correct order:

1. c 2. e 3. a 4. f 5. b 6. d

Words to describe Leopard:
hungry, spotty

Words to describe Zebra:
cheeky, stripy